characters created by laure ild

I would LIKE to
actually keep it

Grosset & Dunlap
An Imprint of Penguin Group (USA) Inc.

Charlie and Lola™

Text based on the script written by David Ingham.

Illustrations from the TV animations produced by Tiger Aspect

GROSSET & DUNLAP
Published by the Penguin Group
Penguin Group (USA) Inc., 375 Hudson Street, New York, New York 10014, USA
Penguin Group (Canada), 90 Eglinton Avenue East, Suite 700, Toronto, Ontario M4P 2Y3, Canada
(a division of Pearson Penguin Canada Inc.)
Penguin Books Ltd., 80 Strand, London WC2R 0RL, England
Penguin Group Ireland, 25 St. Stephen's Green, Dublin 2, Ireland
(a division of Penguin Books Ltd.)
Penguin Group (Australia), 250 Camberwell Road, Camberwell, Victoria 3124, Australia
(a division of Pearson Australia Group Pty. Ltd.)
Penguin Books India Pvt. Ltd., 11 Community Centre, Panchsheel Park, New Delhi—110 017, India
Penguin Group (NZ), 67 Apollo Drive, Rosedale, North Shore 0632, New Zealand
(a division of Pearson New Zealand Ltd.)
Penguin Books (South Africa) (Pty.) Ltd., 24 Sturdee Avenue,
Rosebank, Johannesburg 2196, South Africa

Penguin Books Ltd., Registered Offices: 80 Strand, London WC2R 0RL, England

ISBN 978-0-448-45678-2   10 9 8

I have this little sister, Lola.
She is small and very funny.
Lola really loves her **toy fox**.

Lola says,
"Don't let your egg
go all freezing and cold, Foxy."

"Can
you
do some
more
pushing,
Foxy?"

"Now, Foxy, we can count sheep . . .

one,

two,

three . . ."

Lola loves Foxy so much,
she takes him
almost
everywhere.

On the way to school,
Lola says,
"Look, an actual toy rabbit.
I should take it
            to school."

"It looks so lonely,"
says Lotta.

        I say, "We should
leave it here on the wall.
            Then whoever
lost the rabbit can
come back here to find it."

At lunch Lola says,
"I am still slightly worrying
about Rabbit."

And Lotta says,
"I'm sure someone
will come and
get him. He might even be
home by now."

But Lola says,
"What if he isn't?"

"Let's check!"

"What if a bat
takes him to a big, HUGE
cave?" says Lola.

"Or what if a big,
ginormous
bird flies off with him?"
says Lotta.

So I say,
"He's too big for a bird to
carry off, and
bats only come out at
nighttime."

On our way home,
Lola says, "Charlie!
Rabbit is still here!"

So I say,
"Let's take him home."

But Lotta says,
"How are we going to
find out who
Rabbit belongs to?"

And I say,
"I have an idea . . ."

"We can put posters up,"
I say. "And then
Rabbit's owner might
see them and call us."

So Lola, Lotta,
Marv, and I put up posters
everywhere.

Lola says,
"Now what do we do?"

And I say,
"We just have to wait."

At home Lola says,
"Has anyone called yet?"

And I say,
"Lola, we only just put up
the posters."

And she says,
"Charlie, somebody
will call soon, won't they?"

And I say, "I'm
sure they will."

"Don't worry, Rabbit.
We will find your
home," says Lola.

Lola takes very good
care of **Rabbit**.

She brushes his teeth.

She gives him tea.

"Time for tea!"

And even cuddles
with him at night.

The next day,
Lola says,
    "It's been ages, Charlie.
What if no one ever calls?
    What will we do then?"

"I guess you can keep
Rabbit," I say.

"Really?" says Lola.

"Yes," I say.
"But I'm sure
        someone will call."

A bit later,
the phone rings.

I say, "Hello . . .
yes, it's a blue rabbit . . .
yes, we will
wait for you to come
and collect it."

"Lola!" I say.
"Rabbit's owner is coming
to get him now."

"But I really like Rabbit,"
says Lola.

So I say, "But, Lola,
he isn't yours.
The boy who owns Rabbit
wants him back."

Then the doorbell rings.

"Hoppy!" says the boy.
"It's Hoppy!"

And Lola says,
"I absolutely looked
             after him for you."

And he says,
"Thank you. Thank you
             very much."

Lola says, "I will miss **Rabbit**
very much. But Foxy won't.
    He said **Rabbit** kept stealing
the blankets."